Spelling and Writing

MW01321520

Table of Contents

Glossary 2
Spelling: Spelling word with ie and ei 3
Writing: Writing four kinds of sentences 4
Spelling: Figuring out homophones 5
Writing: Writing directions 6
Writing: Putting ideas together 7
Spelling: Spelling some tough words 8
Review 9
Spelling: Spelling words with /ûr/ and /ôr/ 10
Writing: Using similes and metaphors 11
Spelling: Searching for synonyms 12
Writing: Creating word pictures 13
Spelling: Using different forms of verbs 14
Writing: Describing people 15
Spelling: Spelling plurals 16
Review 17
Spelling: Spelling with /kw/, /ks/, and /gz/ 18
Writing: Writing free verse 19
Spelling: Analyzing words and their parts 20
Writing: Writing limericks 21
Spelling: Figuring out a crossword puzzle 22
Writing: Writing acrostics 23
Spelling: Finding the spelling mistakes 24
Review 25
Spelling: Spelling words with silent letters 26
Writing: Organizing paragraphs 27
Writing: Building paragraphs 28
Spelling: Matching subjects and verbs 29
Writing: Explaining with examples 30
Spelling: Making nouns possessive 31
Review 32

Copyright © 1994 American Education Publishing Co.

Spelling and Writing

Glossary

Adjective. A word that discribes nouns.
Adverb. A word that tells something about a verb.
Analogy. Shows a relationship between two pairs of words.
Apostrophe. A punctuation mark that shows possession (Kim's hat) or takes the place of missing letters in a word (isn't).
Consonants. All the letters except **a, e, i, o, u,** and sometimes **y**.
Fact. A true statement. Something that can be proved.
Homophones. Words that sound alike but have different spellings and meanings.
Joining Words (Conjunctions). Words that join sentences or combine ideas: **and, but, or, because, when, after, so**.
Metaphor. A comparison of two unlike things without the words **like** or **as**.
Noun. A word that names a person, place, or thing.
Opinion. What someone thinks or believes.
Paragraph. A group of sentences that tells about one main idea.
Plural. A word that refers to more than one thing, such as a plural noun or verb.
Possessive Noun. A noun that owns something, such as **Jill's** book or the **women's** hair.
Prefix. One or two syllables added to the beginning of a word to change its meaning.
Pronoun. Words that can be used in place if a noun, such as **I, she, it,** and **them**.
Question. A sentence that asks something.
Simile. A comparison of two unlike things using the words **like** or **as**.
Singular. A word that refers to only one thing, such as a singular noun or verb.
Statement. A sentence that tells something.
Subject. A word or several words that tell whom or what a sentence is about.
Suffix. One or two syllables added to the end of a word.
Syllable. A word—or part of a word—with only one vowel sound.
Synonym. A word that means the same thing as another word.
Verb. The action word in a sentence; the word that tells what something does or that something exists.

Spelling Words With ie And ei

Many people have trouble deciding whether to spell a word **ie** or **ei**, with good reason. The following rules have many exceptions, but they may be helpful to you. If the two letters are pronounced /ē/ and are preceded by an /s/ sound, spell them **ei**, as in rec**ei**ve. If the two letters are pronounced /ē/ but are not preceded by an /s/ sound, spell them **ie** as in bel**ie**ve. If the letters are pronounced /ā/, spell them **eigh** as in **eigh**t or **ei** as in v**ei**n. If the letters are pronounced /ī/, spell them **eigh** then, too, as in h**eigh**t.

Directions: Use the words from the word box in these exercises.

veil	brief	deceive	belief	niece
vein	reindeer	yield	achieve	height
neighbor	seize	grief	ceiling	weight

1. Write each word in the row that names at least one of its vowel sounds. (One word will be listed twice.)

/sē/ _____

/ē/ _____

/ā/ _____

/ī/ _____

2. Finish each sentence with a word that has the vowel sound given. Use each word from the word box only once.

My next-door /ā/ _____ wore a long /ā/ _____ at her wedding.

Will the roof hold the /ā/ _____ of Santa's /ā/ _____ ?

My nephew and /ē/ _____ work hard to /ē/ _____ their goals.

I have a strong /ē/ _____ they would never /ē/ _____ me.

For a /ē/ _____ moment, I thought Tim would /ē/ _____ the game to me.

The blood rushed through my /ā/ _____ .

What is the /ī/ _____ of this /ē/ _____ ?

The thief was going to /ē/ _____ the money!

Spelling and Writing

Name: _____

Writing Four Kinds Of Sentences

Remember the four main kinds of sentences:
- A **statement** tells something.
- A **question** asks something.
- A **command** tells someone to do something.
- An **exclamation** shows surprise or excitement.

Directions: Write what you might say in each situation below. Then tell whether the sentence you wrote was a statement, question, command, or exclamation. Write at least one of each. Be sure to use periods after statements and commands, question marks after questions, and exclamation marks after exclamations.

FOUR KINDS OF SENTENCES.

Like this:
Write what you might say to a friend who's late to school:

<u>Why are you late?</u>   question

<u>Boy, are you in trouble!</u>   exclamation

Write what you might say to:

1. A friend who studied all night for the math test

   _____

2. Your teacher about yesterday's homework

   _____

3. A child you're watching who won't sit still for a brief second

   _____

4. Your sister, who's been on the phone too long

   _____

5. A strange kid who just seized your bike

   _____

6. A friend who's carrying a big box

   _____

7. Your dad, who's trying to lose weight

   _____

8. A friend who's been teasing you about your height

   _____

Copyright © 1994 American Education Publishing Co.

Spelling and Writing Name: _____

Figuring Out Homophones

Homophones are two words that sound the same, but have different spellings and different meanings. Here are several homophones: night/knight, fair/fare, not/knot.

Directions: Finish each sentence with the correct homophone. Then write another sentence using the other homophone in the pair.

Like this:

    Eight/ate   So far I <u>ate</u> two cookies.

                 Joanie had <u>eight</u> cookies!

1. Vein/vain
   Since the newspaper printed his picture, Andy has been so self-centered and _____.
   _____

2. Weight/wait
   We had to _____ a long time for the show to start.
   _____

3. Weigh/way
   He always insists that we do it his _____.
   _____

4. Seize/seas
   The explorers charted the _____.
   _____

Directions: Write each word from the word box next to the way it's pronounced.

veil	brief	deceive	belief	niece
vein	reindeer	yield	achieve	height
neighbor	seize	grief	ceiling	weight

/bēlēf/ _____ /sēz/ _____ /nābər/ _____

/vāl/ _____ /rāndēr/ _____ /hīt/ _____

/wāt/ _____ /yēld/ _____ /grēf/ _____

/sēling/ _____ /dēsēv/ _____ /brēf/ _____

/achēv/ _____ /nēs/ _____ /vān/ _____

Spelling and Writing Name: _____

Writing Directions

Directions must be clearly written. They are easiest to follow when they are in numbered steps. Each direction should start with a verb, like these:

How to peel a banana
1. Hold the banana by the stem end.
2. Find a loose edge of peel at the top.
3. Pull the peel down.
4. Peel the other sections of the banana in the same way.

Directions: Rewrite these directions so the steps are in order, are numbered, and start with verbs.

How to feed a dog

Finally, call the dog to come and eat. Then you carry the filled dish to the place where the dog eats. The can or bag should be opened by you. First, clean the dog's food dish with soap and water. Then get the dogfood out of the cupboard. Put the right amount of food in the dish.

_____
_____
_____
_____
_____
_____

Directions:
1. On another sheet of paper, draw two symbols, such as a square with a star in one corner or a triangle inside a circle. Don't show your drawing to anybody.
2. On a different sheet of paper, write instructions that someone else could follow to make the same drawing. Make sure your instructions are clear, in order, numbered, and start with verbs.
3. Copy them below.
4. Trade instructions (but not pictures) with a partner. See if you can follow each other's instructions to make the drawings.
5. Show your partner the drawing you made in step one. Does it look like the one he or she made following your instructions? Could you follow your partner's instructions? Share what was clear—or not so clear—about each other's instructions.

Putting Ideas Together

We join two sentences with **and** when they are more or less equal:
   Julie is coming, **and** she is bringing cookies.

We join two sentences with **but** when the second sentence contradicts the first one:
   Julie is coming, **but** she will be late.

We join two sentences with **or** when they name a choice:
   Julie might bring cookies, **or** she might bring a cake.

We join two sentences with **because** when the second one names the reason for the first one:
   I'll bring cookies, too, **because** Julie might forget hers.

We join two sentences with **so** when the second one names a result of the first one:
   Julie is bringing cookies, **so** we won't starve.

Directions: Finish each sentence with an idea that fits with the first part.

Like this:
   We could watch TV, or _we could play Monopoly._

1. I wanted to seize the opportunity, but _____

2. You had better not deceive me because _____

3. My neighbor was on vacation, so _____

4. Veins take blood back to your heart, and _____

5. You can't always yield to your impulses because _____

6. I know that is your belief, but _____

7. It could be reindeer on the roof, or _____

8. Brent was determined to achieve his goal, so _____

9. Brittany was proud of her height because _____

10. We painted the ceiling, and _____

Spelling Some Tough Words

Directions: Write in the missing letters in the words below. If you have trouble, look in the word box on page 3.

Some people are dec____ved into thinking that r____ndeer aren't real. Actually, r____ndeer live in colder areas of North America and other parts of the world. They reach a h____ght of 2.3-4.6 feet at the shoulder. Their w____ght may be 600 pounds. When the males battle, one of them y____lds to the other.

My n____ghbor had a stroke. One of his v____ns burst in his brain, so now he has trouble walking. Instead of being overcome with gr____f, he exercises every day so he can ach____ve his goal of walking again. I have a strong bel____f that some day soon I will see him walking all by himself.

Directions: Only one word in each sentence below is misspelled. Write it correctly on the line.

1. Fierce wolves hunt the raindeer. _____

2. My neice wore a long veil at her wedding. _____

3. My nieghbor is trying to lose weight. _____

4. Everyone gives me greif about my height. _____

5. His neighbor's house is beyond beleif. _____

6. The vain of gold yielded a pound of nuggets. _____

7. Trying to acheive too much can lead to grief. _____

8. She decieved us about how much weight she lost. _____

9. His niece is tall enough to reach the cieling. _____

10. A vale of water fell from a great height. _____

11. "That sign said, 'Yeeld,'" the officer pointed out. _____

12. The worker siezed the box, despite its weight. _____

Spelling and Writing Name: _____

Review

Directions: Follow the instructions below to see how much you remember from the previous lessons. Can you finish this page correctly without looking back at the other lessons?

1. Write three words that spell /ā/ with ei. _____

2. Write a word that spells /ī/ with ei. _____

3. Write two words that spell /ē/ with ei. _____

4. Write a statement with one subject, two verbs, and an adverb. Mark them S, V, and ADV.

   _____

5. Write a question with two subjects, one verb, and an adjective. Mark them S, V, and ADJ.

   _____

6. Use the homophone for sealing in a command:

   _____

7. Use the word pronounced /nēs/ in an exclamation:

   _____

8. Finish these sentences in ways that make sense:

   The ceiling fell down, but _____

   The ceiling fell down because _____

   The ceiling fell down, so _____

9. Find three misspelled words and write them correctly.

   Todd breefly decieved me about what he was trying to acheive.

   _____

Spelling and Writing   Name: _____

Spelling Words With /ûr/ And /ôr/

The difference between /ûr/ and /ôr/ is clear in the difference between f**ur** and f**or**.

The /ûr/ sound can be spelled **ur** as in f**ur**, **our** as in j**our**nal, **er** as in h**er**, and **ear** as in s**ear**ch.

The /ôr/ sound can be spelled **or** as in f**or**, **our** as in f**our**, **oar** as in s**oar**, and **ore** as in m**ore**.

Directions: Use words from the word box in these exercises.

florist	courtesy	research	emergency	flourish
plural	observe	furnish	tornado	source
ignore	survey	normal	coarse	restore

1. Write each word in the row that names a sound in it.

/ûr/ _____
_____

/ôr/ _____
_____

2. Finish each sentence with a word that has the sound given. Use each word from the word box only once.

We all get along better when we remember to use /ûr/ _____.

My brother likes flowers and wants to be a /ôr/ _____.

What was the /ôr/ _____ of

the /ûr/ _____ for your report?

For a plural subject, use a /ûr/ _____ verb.

He waved at her, but she continued to /ôr/ _____ him.

Beneath the dark clouds was a /ôr/ _____ !

Firefighters are used to handling an /ûr/ _____.

When will they be able to /ôr/ _____ our electricity?

How are you going to /ûr/ _____ your apartment?

Copyright © 1994 American Education Publishing Co.

Spelling and Writing   Name: _____

Using Similes And Metaphors

A **simile** compares two unlike things using the words **like** or **as**.
   For example: The fog was like a blanket around us.

A **metaphor** compares two unlike things without the words **like** or **as**.
   For example: The fog was a blanket around us.

"The fog was thick" is not a simile or a metaphor. "Thick" is just an adjective. Similes and metaphors compare two unlike things.

Directions: In each sentence, underline the two unlike things being compared. Then mark the sentence **S** for simile or **M** for metaphor.

_____ 1. The florist's shop was a summer garden.

_____ 2. The wood was as coarse as sandpaper.

_____ 3. The survey was a fountain of information.

_____ 4. Her courtesy was as welcome as a cool breeze on a hot day.

_____ 5. The room was like a furnace.

Directions: Finish these sentences with similes.

1. The tornado was as dark as _____

2. His voice was like _____

3. The emergency was as unexpected as _____

4. The kittens were like _____

Directions: Finish these sentences with metaphors.

1. To me, research was _____

2. The flourishing plants were _____

3. My observation at the hospital was _____

4. Her ignoring me was _____

Spelling and Writing

Searching For Synonyms

Directions: In each sentence, find a word or group of words that is a synonym for a word in the word box. Circle the word(s) and write the synonym on the line.

florist	courtesy	research	emergency	flourish
plural	observe	furnish	tornado	source
ignored	survey	normally	coarse	restore

1. The children seemed to thrive in their new school. _____

2. Her politeness made me feel welcome. _____

3. The flower shop was closed when we arrived. _____

4. The principal came to watch our class. _____

5. Are they going to fix up that old house? _____

6. Six weeks after the tornado, the neighborhood looked the same as it usually did. _____

7. What was the origin of that rumor? _____

8. The windstorm destroyed two houses. _____

9. She neglected her homework. _____

10. The material had a rough feeling to it. _____

11. Did you fill out your questionnaire yet? _____

Directions: Pick three of the words below and write a sentence for each one, showing you know what the word means. Then trade sentences with someone. Do you think your partner understands the words he or she used in sentences?

plural	flourish	source	restore	observe	furnish

1. _____
2. _____
3. _____

Creating Word Pictures

Directions: Rewrite each general sentence below two times, giving two different versions of what the sentence could mean. Be sure to use more specific nouns and verbs and add adjectives and adverbs. Similes and metaphors will also help create a picture with words. Notice how much more interesting and informative the two rewritten sentences are in this example:

The animal ate its food.
<u>Like a hungry lion, the starving cocker spaniel wolfed down the entire bowl of food in seconds.</u>
<u>The raccoon delicately washed the berries in the stream before nibbling them slowly, one by one.</u>

1. The person built something.
_____
_____

2. The weather was bad.
_____
_____

3. The boy went down the street.
_____
_____

4. The helpers helped.
_____
_____

5. The bird flew to the tree.
_____
_____

Spelling and Writing

Name: _____

Using Different Forms Of Verbs

To explain what is happening right now, we can use a "plain" verb or we can use **is** or **are** and add **-ing** to a verb.
Like this: We enjoy. They are enjoying.

To explain something that already happened, we can add **-ed** to many verbs or we can use **was** or **were** and add **-ing** to a verb.
Like this: He surveyed. The workers were surveying.

Remember to drop the final **e** on verbs before adding another ending and to add **-es** instead of just **-s** to verbs that end with **sh** or **ch**.
Like this: She is restoring. He furnishes.

Directions: Finish each sentence with the correct form of the verb given. Some sentences already have **is**, **are**, **was**, or **were**.

1. The florist is (have) a sale this week. _____

2. Last night's tornado (destroy) a barn. _____

3. We are (research) the history of our town. _____

4. My mistake was (use) a plural verb instead of a singular one. _____

5. She (act) quickly in yesterday's emergency. _____

6. Our group is (survey) the parents in our community. _____

7. For our last experiment, we (observe) a plant's growth for two weeks. _____

8. A local company already (furnish) all of the materials for this project. _____

9. Which dairy (furnish) milk to our cafeteria every day? _____

10. Just (ignore) the mess in here. _____

11. I get so angry when he (ignore) me. _____

12. Our town is (restore) some old buildings. _____

13. This fern grows and (flourish) in our bathroom. _____

14. Well, it was (flourish) until I overwatered it. _____

Spelling and Writing   Name: _____

Describing People

Directions: Often we can show our readers how someone feels by describing how that person looks or what he or she is doing. Read the phrases below. Write in a word or two to show how you think that person feels.

1. Like a tornado, yelling, raised fists: _____
2. Slumped, walking slowing, head down: _____
3. Trembling, breathing quickly, like a cornered animal: _____

Directions: Write two or three sentences to describe how each person below feels. Don't name any emotions, such as angry, excited, or frightened. Instead, tell how the person looks and what he or she is doing. Create a picture with specific nouns and verbs, plus adjectives, adverbs, similes, and metaphors.

1. a runner who has just won a race for his or her school

   _____

   _____

2. someone on the first day in a new school

   _____

   _____

3. someone walking down the street and spotting a house on fire

   _____

   _____

4. a scientist who has just discovered a cure for lung cancer

   _____

   _____

5. a person being ignored by his or her best friend

   _____

   _____

Copyright © 1994 American Education Publishing Co.

Spelling Plurals

Is it hero**s** or hero**es**? Many people aren't sure. Although these rules have exceptions, they will help you spell the plural forms of words that end with **o**:
 If a word ends with a consonant and **o**, add **-es**: hero**es**.
 If a word ends with a vowel and **o**, just add **-s**: radio**s**.
Don't forget other rules for plurals:
 If a word ends with **s**, **ss**, **z**, **x**, **ch**, or **sh**, add **-es**:
 buses, classes, quizzes, taxes, peaches, wishes.
 if a word ends with **f** or **fe**, drop the **f** or **fe** and add **-ves**:
 leaf, leaves; wife, wives.
 Some plurals don't end with **-s** or **-es**: geese, deer, children.
 The **-es** rule also applies when a word ending with
 s, **ss**, **z**, **x**, **ch**, or **sh** is used as a verb:
 kisses, mixes, teaches, pushes.

Directions: Write in the plural forms of the words given.

1. Our area doesn't often have (tornado). _____

2. How many (radio) does this store sell every month? _____

3. (Radish) are the same color as apples. _____

4. Does this submarine carry (torpedo)? _____

5. Hawaii has a number of active (volcano). _____

6. Did you pack (knife) in the picnic basket? _____

7. We heard (echo) when we shouted in the canyon. _____

8. Where is the list of (address) ? _____

Directions: Write the correct verb forms in these sentences.

1. What will you do when that plant (reach) the ceiling? _____

2. Sometimes my dad (fix) us milkshakes. _____

3. Every night my sister (wish) on the first star she sees. _____

4. Who (furnish) the school with pencils and paper? _____

5. The author (research) every detail in her books. _____

ANSWER KEY

This Answer Key has been designed so that it may be easily removed if you so desire.

GRADE 6 READING COMPREHENSION

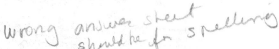
wrong answer sheet should be for spelling

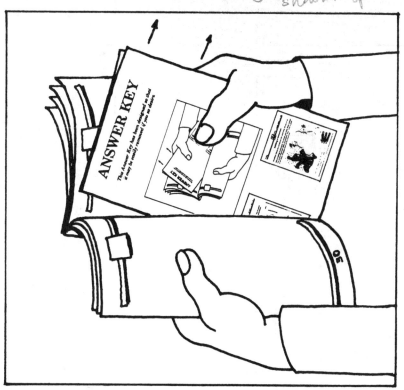

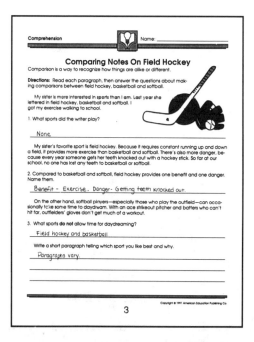

Comparing Notes On Field Hockey

1. What sports did the writer play?
   None.

2. Compared to basketball and softball, field hockey provides one benefit and one danger. Name them.
   Benefit - Exercise. Danger - Getting teeth knocked out.

3. What sports **do not** allow time for daydreaming?
   Field hockey and basketball

Write a short paragraph telling which sport you like best and why.
   Paragraphs vary.

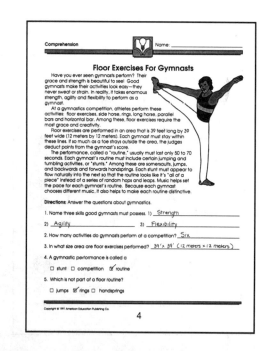

Floor Exercises For Gymnasts

1. Name three skills good gymnasts must possess. 1) Strength 2) Agility 3) Flexibility

2. How many activities do gymnasts perform at a competition? Six

3. In what size area are floor exercises performed? 39' x 39' (12 meters x 12 meters)

4. A gymnastic performance is called a
   ☐ stunt ☐ competition ☒ routine

5. Which is not part of a floor routine?
   ☐ jumps ☒ rings ☐ handsprings

Fact Or Opinion?

A fact can be proved. An opinion, which cannot be proved, tells what someone believes.

Directions: Read the numbered sentences and put an x in the corresponding numbered boxes to tell whether each sentence gives a fact or an opinion.

1. Gymnasts are the most exciting athletes to watch!
2. Because their sport requires all-over body strength, gymnasts must have very strong arms and legs. Their stomach muscles and the muscles in their feet must also be in good condition.
3. To do handstands, gymnasts must support the weight of their upside-down bodies by holding their hands flat and their arms straight. Their legs must be pointed straight up.
4. With a little practice, I think anyone could learn to do a handstand.
5. A somersault is more difficult than a handstand.
6. It requires starting and stopping from a standing position after making a 360-degree turn in the air.
7. I'll bet not many people can do a good somersault!
8. Some of the different kinds of somersaults are backwards somersaults, sideways somersaults and something called a "bent body" somersault.
9. I've never seen a bent body somersault, but I think it must require a lot of bending.
10. I don't think I would be any good at the bent body somersault.

1. ☐ Fact ☒ Opinion
2. ☒ Fact ☐ Opinion
3. ☒ Fact ☐ Opinion
4. ☐ Fact ☒ Opinion
5. ☐ Fact ☒ Opinion
6. ☒ Fact ☐ Opinion
7. ☐ Fact ☒ Opinion
8. ☒ Fact ☐ Opinion
9. ☐ Fact ☒ Opinion
10. ☐ Fact ☒ Opinion

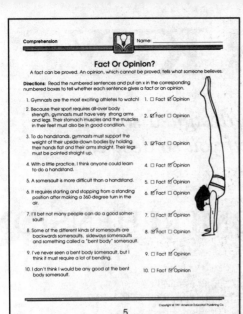

Comparing Gymnastics Exercises

Directions: Read each paragraph, then answer the questions about making comparisons between ring stunts and floor exercises.

1. Ring stunts and floor exercises in gymnastics require different kinds of skills. The most obvious difference between the two is that the feet touch the floor in floor exercises.

What do the feet touch in ring stunts? __Nothing__

2. Both floor exercises and ring stunts require graceful movement and the ability to move smoothly from one stunt to another. Ring stunts require great strength in the arms and shoulders. Floor exercises require the gymnast to be sure-footed.

Do floor exercises require great arm and shoulder strength?
__No__

3. Do ring stunts (prior to dismounting) require the gymnast to be sure-footed? __No__

4. Because they tend to have stronger upper bodies, men do better in ring exercises than women. However, many spectators insist that women are more exciting performers of floor exercises.

Compared to men, what do women excel at in gymnastics? __Floor exercises__

5. Because of their smaller size, Japanese men frequently outperform American men on ring stunts. Perhaps because they tend to have longer legs to swing around, American men find mastering ring stunts more of a challenge. This comparison does not hold true for floor exercises.

What factor seems to have no bearing on excelling at floor exercises?
__Small size__

Warming Up To Gymnastics

Because no bats, racquets or balls are used, some people mistakenly believe that gymnastics is not a dangerous sport. Although major injuries don't happen often, broken legs—as well as broken necks and backs—can occur. The reason they don't happen frequently is that gymnasts follow safety rules that help prevent accidents.

One thing gymnasts are careful to do every time they practice their sport is to first warm up their muscles. "Warm-ups" are exercises that gently stretch and loosen the muscles before subjecting them to tension and strain.

Warm-ups help the muscles gradually expand and stretch so they move efficiently during vigorous exercise. Without a warm-up of 15 to 30 minutes it's possible that unworked muscles will be dangerously pulled or strained. Because a muscle injury can interfere with—or stop—an athlete's performance, experienced gymnasts never skip or rush through their warm-ups.

Another thing gymnasts do to help prevent accidents is to use "spotters" when they practice. Spotters are people—usually other gymnasts—who stand beside gymnasts when they are practicing new movements. If gymnasts twist the wrong way or begin to fall, spotters will grab them to prevent injury. Spotters also often offer helpful advice and instant feedback on gymnasts' performances.

Directions: Answer the questions about gymnastics.

1. Name two things gymnasts can do to prevent accidents.
1) __warm up__ 2) __use spotters__

2. What's the purpose of a warm-up?
__Helps muscles gradually expand and stretch.__

3. Name three things spotters can do to help gymnasts.
1) __Grab them to prevent injuries__ 2) __offer helpful advice__ 3) __offer instant feedback__

4. Which is not a good length of time for gymnasts to warm up?
☒ 5 minutes ☐ 15 minutes ☐ 30 minutes

5. Which is the least likely injury to happen to a gymnast?
☐ broken leg ☐ broken back ☒ broken head

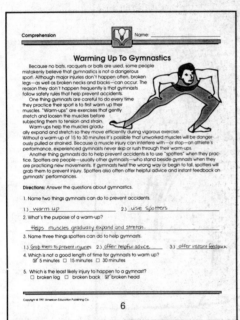

Review

When gymnastics became popular at the beginning of this century, ring stunts requiring great strength were the most admired routines. Half a century later after World War II, ring routines grew to include swinging stunts as well. Today, performance on rings is divided into two categories. The first category includes stunts that emphasize strength, such as holding the legs out straight while pushing the body up with the arms. In the second category are swinging stunts which display quick and graceful movement. Russians were the first gymnasts to perform a swinging stunt on rings. Their performance of "the wheel"—a full body flip—at the 1952 Olympics met with tremendous applause.

As with floor exercises, side horse, long horse, parallel bars and the horizontal bar, mastery of the rings requires a lot of practice. The final goal of all gymnastics routines is to combine a variety of moves and stunts into a performance that shows strength, flexibility and creativity.

Directions: Answer the questions about gymnastics.

1. Compare ring stunts at the turn of the century to gymnastics after World War II.
__There were not swinging stunts before WWII.__

2. Compared to the Russians, what did the other gymnasts at the 1952 Olympics lack?
__The ability to do swinging stunts__

3. What stunts are in the second category of ring stunts? __Swinging stunts__

4. Name six types of stunts.
1) __Ring__ 2) __floor exercises__ 3) __side horse__
4) __long horse__ 5) __parallel bars__ 6) __horizontal bar__

Fact or opinion?

5. Russians are the best gymnasts in the world. 1. ☐ Fact ☒ Opinion
6. The Russians were the first to perform swinging stunts. 2. ☒ Fact ☐ Opinion

---

Ring Stunts For Gymnasts

Gymnasts who excel at ring stunts must have very strong arms and shoulders. However, gymnastics coaches warn against weight lifting as a way of preparing for using the rings.

Why? Because ring stunts require a delicate combination of balance, coordination and strength. Muscular strength alone is not enough. Coaches say those who first build their muscles weight lifting tend to rely too much on strength and not enough on balance. As a result, their ring performances are not very graceful.

When doing ring stunts gymnasts must support their entire weight with their arms. If you think this is easy, try doing 10 chin-ups in a row on monkey bars. After number three—if you get that far—you will become a respectful admirer of ring stunts.

An especially hard ring stunt is called the "wheel." While hanging from the rings, the gymnast turns his body in a full 360 degree circle—a slow "flip." Another very hard stunt is the "hang swing out." In this stunt, the gymnast gets in a handstand position on the rings, then swings down and out by bending and stretching his hips.

At the end of a ring routine, which includes several stunts, a gymnast often gets off the rings via a "somersault dismount." As he hits the peak of the upward movements of a forward swing, he does a somersault in the air before landing with both feet on the floor. The somersault dismount provides a dramatic conclusion to a gymnast's amazingly graceful show of strength and coordination.

Directions: Answer the questions about ring stunts.

1. Why do coaches warn against weight training for ring stunts?
__To prevent too much reliance on strength and not enough on balance.__

2. Which ring stunt requires a gymnast to turn in a 360 degree circle?
__Wheel__

3. Which is not a ring stunt?
☐ hang swing out ☐ wheel ☒ shoulder swing out

4. In the hang swing out, the gymnast first
☒ gets in a handstand position ☐ gets in a wheel position

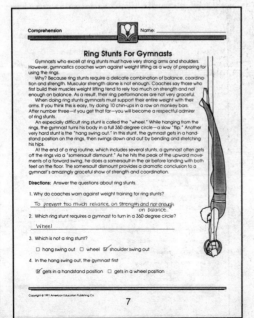

The Ant And The Cricket

A silly young cricket who decided to sing—
Through the warm sunny months of summer and spring
Began to complain when he found that at home
His **cupboards** were empty and winter had come.

At last by starvation the cricket made bold
To hop through the wintertime snow and the cold
Away he set off to a **miserly** ant
To see if to keep him alive he would **grant**;
Shelter from rain, a mouthful of grain.
"I wish only to borrow—I'll repay it tomorrow—
If not, I must die of starvation and sorrow!"

Said the ant to the cricket, "It's true I'm your friend,
But we ants never borrow, we ants never lend.
We ants store up crumbs so when winter arrives
We have just enough food to keep ants alive."

Directions: Answer the questions about the poem.

1. Use context clues to choose the correct definition of "cupboards."
☐ where books are stored ☒ where food is stored ☐ where shoes are stored

2. Use context clues to choose the correct definition of "miserly."
☒ selfish/stingy ☐ generous/kind ☐ mean/ugly

3. Use context clue to choose the correct definition of "grant."
☐ to take away ☐ to belch ☒ to give

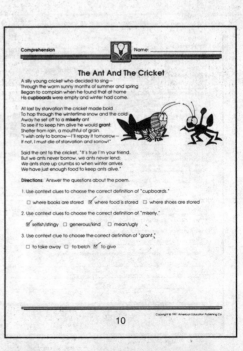

Limericks

Old Man From Peru

There was an old man from Peru
Who dreamed he was eating his shoe.
In the midst of the night
He awoke in a fright
And—good grief!—it was perfectly true.

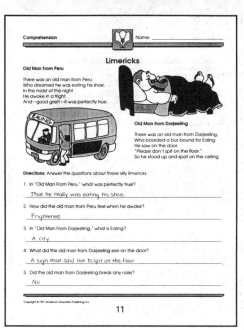

Old Man from Darjeeling

There was an old man from Darjeeling,
Who boarded a bus bound for Ealing.
He saw on the door:
"Please don't spit on the floor."
So he stood up and spat on the ceiling.

Directions: Answer the questions about these silly limericks.

1. In "Old Man From Peru," what was perfectly true?
   That he really was eating his shoe.
2. How did the old man from Peru feel when he awoke?
   Frightened
3. In "Old Man From Darjeeling," what is Ealing?
   A city
4. What did the old man from Darjeeling see on the door?
   A sign that said not to spit on the floor
5. Did the old man from Darjeeling break any rules?
   No

Tree Toad

A tree toad loved a she-toad
Who lived up in a tree.
He was a two-toed tree toad
But a three-toed toad was she.
The two-toed tree toad tried to win
The three-toed she-toad's heart,
For the two-toed tree toad loved her—
She was lovely, kind and smart.
But the two-toed tree toad loved in vain.
He couldn't coax her down
She stayed alone up in the tree
While he cried on the ground.

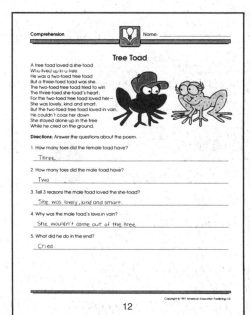

Directions: Answer the questions about the poem.

1. How many toes did the female toad have?
   Three
2. How many toes did the male toad have?
   Two
3. Tell 3 reasons the male toad loved the she-toad?
   She was lovely, kind and smart.
4. Why was the male toad's love in vain?
   She wouldn't come out of the tree.
5. What did he do in the end?
   Cried.

Three Silly Poems

Poem #1

I eat my peas with honey.
I've done it all my life.
It makes the peas taste funny,
But it keeps them on my knife!

Poem #2

At a restaurant that was quite new
A man found a mouse in his stew.
Said the waiter, "Don't shout
Or wave it about,
Or the rest will be wanting one, too!"

Poem #3

If all the world were paper
And all the seas were ink,
And all the trees were bread and cheese,
What would the people think?

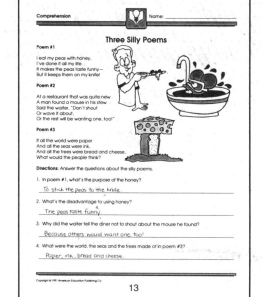

Directions: Answer the questions about the silly poems.

1. In poem #1, what's the purpose of the honey?
   To stick the peas to the knife.
2. What's the disadvantage of using honey?
   The peas taste funny.
3. Why did the waiter tell the diner not to shout about the mouse he found?
   Because others would want one, too!
4. What were the world, the seas and the trees made of in poem #3?
   Paper, ink, bread and cheese.

I Saw A Ship A-Sailing

I saw a ship a-sailing,
A-sailing on the sea.
And, oh! it was all loaded
With tasty things for me.

There was candy in the cabin
And apples in the **hold**;
The sails were made of silk
The **masts** were made of gold.

The four-and-twenty sailors
That stood between the decks,
Were four-and-twenty white mice
With chains around their necks.

The captain was a duck,
With a **packet** on his back.
And when the ship began to move,
The captain said, "Quack! Quack!"

Directions: Answer the questions about the poem.

1. Use context clues to choose the correct definition of "hold."
   ☑ a place inside a ship ☐ to squeeze or hug ☐ a tear or rip
2. Use context clues to choose the correct definition of "masts."
   ☐ scarves covering the face ☑ beams holding up a ship's sails
3. Use context clues to choose the correct definition of "packet."
   ☐ neck chain ☑ backpack ☐ two sails

Old Gaelic Lullaby

Hush! The waves are rolling in
White with foam, white with foam,
Father works amid the din.
But baby sleeps at home.

Hush! The winds roar hoarse and deep—
On they come, on they come!
Brother seek the wandering sheep,
But baby sleeps at home.

Hush! The rain sweeps over the fields
Where cattle roam, where cattle roam.
Sister goes to seek the cows
But baby sleeps at home.

Directions: Answer the questions about the Gaelic lullaby. (A Gaelic lullaby is an ancient Irish or Scottish song some parents sing as they rock their babies to sleep.)

1. What is father doing while baby sleeps?
   Working
2. What is brother doing?
   Looking for lost sheep.
3. What is sister doing?
   Looking for the cows.
4. Is it quiet or noisy while father works?
   ☐ quiet ☑ noisy
5. Which is **not** mentioned in the poem?
   ☐ wind ☑ sunshine ☐ waves ☐ rain

The Lark And The Wren

"Goodnight, Sir Wren!" said the little lark.
"The daylight fades; it will soon be dark.
I've bathed my wings in the sun's last ray.
I've sung my **hymn** to the parting day.
So now I fly to my quiet glen
In **yonder** meadow - Goodnight Wren!"

"Goodnight poor Lark," said the **haughty** wren
With a flick of his wing toward his happy friend.
"I also go to my rest **profound**
But not to sleep on the cold, damp ground.
The fittest place for a bird like me
Is the topmost **bough** of a tall pine tree."

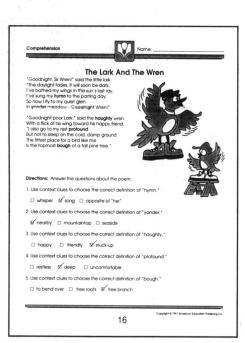

Directions: Answer the questions about the poem.

1. Use context clues to choose the correct definition of "hymn."
   ☐ whisper ☑ song ☐ opposite of "her"
2. Use context clues to choose the correct definition of "yonder."
   ☑ nearby ☐ mountaintop ☐ seaside
3. Use context clues to choose the correct definition of "haughty."
   ☐ happy ☐ friendly ☑ stuck-up
4. Use context clues to choose the correct definition of "profound."
   ☐ restless ☑ deep ☐ uncomfortable
5. Use context clues to choose the correct definition of "bough."
   ☐ to bend over ☐ tree roots ☑ tree branch

The Gettysburg Address

On November 19, 1863, President Abraham Lincoln gave a short speech to dedicate a cemetery of Civil War soldiers in Gettysburg, Pennsylvania where a famous battle was fought. He wrote five drafts of the Gettysburg Address, one of the most stirring speeches of all time. The war ended in 1865.

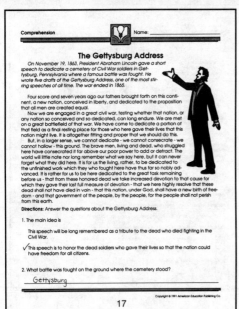

Four score and seven years ago our fathers brought forth on this continent, a new nation, conceived in liberty, and dedicated to the proposition that all men are created equal.

Now we are engaged in a great civil war, testing whether that nation, or any nation so conceived and so dedicated, can long endure. We are met on a great battlefield of that war. We have come to dedicate a portion of that field as a final resting place for those who here gave their lives that this nation might live. It is altogether fitting and proper that we should do this.

But, in a larger sense, we cannot dedicate - we cannot consecrate - we cannot hallow - this ground. The brave men, living and dead, who struggled here have consecrated it far above our poor power to add or detract. The world will little note nor long remember what we say here, but it can never forget what they did here. It is for us the living, rather, to be dedicated to the unfinished work which they who fought here have thus far so nobly advanced. It is rather for us to be here dedicated to the great task remaining before us - that from these honored dead we take increased devotion to that cause for which they gave their last full measure of devotion - that we here highly resolve that these dead shall not have died in vain - that this nation, under God, shall have a new birth of freedom - and that government of the people, by the people, for the people shall not perish from this earth.

Directions: Answer the questions about the Gettysburg Address.

1. The main idea is

☐ This speech will be long remembered as a tribute to the dead who died fighting in the Civil War.

✓ This speech is to honor the dead soldiers who gave their lives so that the nation could have freedom for all citizens.

2. What battle was fought on the ground where the cemetery stood?

Gettysburg

Lincoln And The Southern States

Many people think that Abraham Lincoln had publicly come out against slavery from the beginning of his term as president. This is not the case. Whatever his private feelings, publicly he did not criticize slavery. Fearful that the southern states would secede, or leave, the union, he pledged to respect the southern states' rights to own slaves. He also pledged that the government would respect the southern states' runaway slave laws. These laws required all citizens to return runaway slaves to their masters.

Clearly, Lincoln did not want the country torn apart by a civil war. In the following statement, written in 1861 shortly after he became president, he makes it clear that the federal government will do its best to avoid conflict with the southern states.

I hold that, in contemplation of the universal law and of the Constitution, the Union of these states is perpetual. . . . No state, upon its own mere motion, can lawfully get out of the Union. . . . I shall take care, as the Constitution itself expressly enjoins upon me, that the laws of the Union be faithfully executed in all the states. . . . The power confided to me will be used to hold, occupy, and possess the property and places belonging to the government, and to collect the duties and imposts. . . .

In your hands, my dissatisfied fellow-countrymen, and not in mine, is the momentous issue of civil war. The government will not assail you. You can have no conflict without yourselves being the aggressors. You have no oath registered in heaven to destroy the government, while I shall have the most solemn one to "preserve protect and defend" it.

Directions: Answer the questions about Lincoln and the southern states.

1. Use a dictionary to find the definition of "assail." _Physically attack_

2. Use a dictionary to find the definition of "enjoin." _To order_

3. Use a dictionary to find the definition of "contemplation." _The study of_

4. Lincoln is telling the southern states that the government

☐ does want a war ✓ doesn't want a war ☐ will stop a war

5. As president, Lincoln pledged to "preserve, protect and defend"

☐ slavery ☐ the northern states ✓ the union

The Emancipation Proclamation

On September 22, 1862—a year before delivering the Gettysburg Address President Lincoln delivered The Emancipation Proclamation, which stated that all slaves in Confederate states should be set free. Since the Confederate states had already withdrawn from the Union, they of course ignored the Proclamation. The Proclamation did strengthen the north's war effort. About 200,000 black men—mostly former slaves—enlisted in the Union Army. Two years later the 13th Amendment to the Constitution ended slavery in all parts of the United States.

I, Abraham Lincoln, do order and declare that all persons held as slaves in said designated States and parts of States are, and henceforward shall be, free; and that the Executive Government of the United States, including military and naval authorities thereof, shall recognize and maintain the freedom of said persons.

And I hereby enjoin upon the people so declared to be free to abstain from all violence, unless in necessary self-defense; and I recommend to them that, in all cases where allowed, they labor faithfully for reasonable wages.

And I further declare and make known that such persons of suitable condition will be received into the armed forces of the United States to garrison forts, positions, stations, and other places, and to man vessels of all sorts in said service.

(This is not the full text of the Emancipation Proclamation.)

Directions: Answer the questions about the Emancipation Proclamation.

1. How did the Emancipation Proclamation strengthen the north's war effort?

By allowing black men to join the Union Army - 200,000 of them did

2. Which came first, the Emancipation Proclamation or the Gettysburg Address?

Emancipation Proclamation

3. Which amendment to the constitution grew out of the Emancipation Proclamation?

13th Amendment

Fact Or Opinion?

Directions: Read the numbered sentences and put an x in the corresponding numbered boxes to tell whether each sentence gives a fact or an opinion.

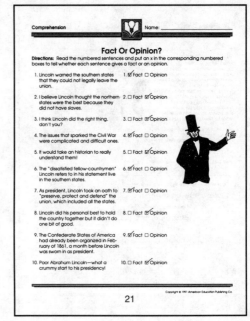

1. Lincoln warned the southern states that they could not legally leave the union.
   1. ✓ Fact ☐ Opinion

2. I believe Lincoln thought the northern states were the best because they did not have slaves.
   2. ☐ Fact ✓ Opinion

3. I think Lincoln did the right thing, don't you?
   3. ☐ Fact ✓ Opinion

4. The issues that sparked the Civil War were complicated and difficult ones.
   4. ✓ Fact ☐ Opinion

5. It would take an historian to really understand them!
   5. ☐ Fact ✓ Opinion

6. The "dissatisfied fellow-countrymen" Lincoln refers to in his statement live in the southern states.
   6. ✓ Fact ☐ Opinion

7. As president, Lincoln took an oath to "preserve, protect and defend" the union, which included all the states.
   7. ✓ Fact ☐ Opinion

8. Lincoln did his personal best to hold the country together but it didn't do one bit of good.
   8. ☐ Fact ✓ Opinion

9. The Confederate States of America had already been organized in February of 1861, a month before Lincoln was sworn in as president.
   9. ✓ Fact ☐ Opinion

10. Poor Abraham Lincoln—what a crummy start to his presidency!
    10. ☐ Fact ✓ Opinion

Puzzling Out The Proclamation

Directions: Use the facts you learned about the Emancipation Proclamation to work the puzzle.

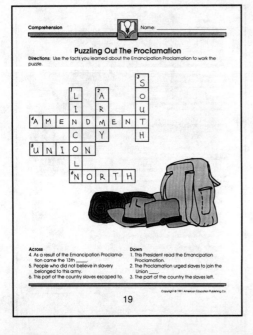

Across
4. As a result of the Emancipation Proclamation came the 13th ____.
5. People who did not believe in slavery belonged to this army.
6. This part of the country slaves escaped to.

Down
1. This President read the Emancipation Proclamation.
2. The Proclamation urged slaves to join the ____ Union.
3. The part of the country the slaves left.

Answers: 1-LINCOLN, 2-ARMY, 3-SOUTH, 4-AMENDMENT, 5-UNION, 6-NORTH

Away Down South In Dixie

Although many southerners disapproved of slavery, the pressure to go along with the majority who supported slavery was very strong. Many of those who thought slavery was wrong did not talk about their opinions. It was dangerous to do so!

The main reason the southern states seceded (withdrew) from the union in 1861 was because they wanted to protect their right to own slaves. They also wanted to increase the number of slaves so they could increase production of cotton and other crops that slaves tended. Many Civil War monuments in the south are dedicated to a war that was described as "just and holy."

"Dixie", a song written in 1859 that is still popular in the south, sums up the attitude of many southerners. As the song lyrics show, southerners' loyalties lay not with the union representing all the states, but with the south and the southern way of life.

Dixie

I wish I was in Dixie, Hoo-ray! Hoo-ray!
In Dixie land I'll take my stand
To live and die in Dixie.
Away, away, away down south in Dixie!
Away, away, away down south in Dixie!

(This is not the full text of the song.)

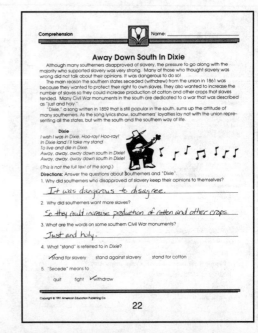

Directions: Answer the questions about Southerners and "Dixie".

1. Why did southerners who disapproved of slavery keep their opinions to themselves?

It was dangerous to disagree.

2. Why did southerners want more slaves?

So they could increase production of cotton and other crops.

3. What are the words on some southern Civil War monuments?

Just and holy.

4. What "stand" is referred to in Dixie?

✓ stand for slavery ☐ stand against slavery ☐ stand for cotton

5. "Secede" means to

☐ quit ☐ fight ✓ withdraw

Fact Or Opinion?

Directions: Read the numbered sentences and put an x in the corresponding numbered boxes to tell whether each sentence gives a fact or an opinion.

1. *Dixie* is a beautiful song! — ☐ Fact ☒ Opinion
2. It was written in 1859 by a man named Daniel Emmett, who died in 1904. — ☒ Fact ☐ Opinion
3. The song became a rallying cry for southerners because it showed where their loyalties were. — ☒ Fact ☐ Opinion
4. I think their loyalty to slavery was absolutely wrong! — ☐ Fact ☒ Opinion
5. These four states where people owned slaves did not secede from the Union: Delaware, Maryland, Kentucky and Missouri. — ☒ Fact ☐ Opinion
6. The people in these states certainly made the right moral choice. — ☐ Fact ☒ Opinion
7. The ownership of one human being by another is absolutely and totally wrong under any circumstances. — ☐ Fact ☒ Opinion
8. In the states that did not secede from the union, some people fought for the Union and others fought for the Confederacy of Southern States. — ☒ Fact ☐ Opinion
9. Sometimes brothers fought against brothers on opposite sides of the war. — ☒ Fact ☐ Opinion
10. What a horrible situation to be in! — ☐ Fact ☒ Opinion

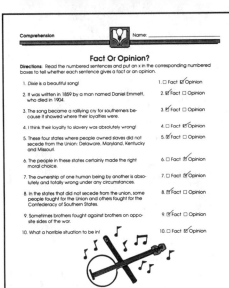

Review

Although they were outnumbered, most southerners were convinced they could win the Civil War. The white population of the southern states was 5.5 million. The population was 18.9 million in the 19 states that stayed with the Union. Despite these odds, southerners felt history was on their side.

After all, the Colonists had been the underdogs against the British and had won the war for independence. Europeans also felt that Lincoln could not force the South to re-join the Union. The United Netherlands had successfully seceded from Spain. Greece had seceded from Turkey. Europeans were laying odds that two countries would take the place of what had once been the United States.

Directions: Answer the questions and work the puzzle.

1. What was the difference in population between the Union and Confederate states? **13.4 million**
2. The main idea is
   ✓ Although they were outnumbered, many people here and abroad felt the South would win the Civil War.
   ☐ Because they were outnumbered, the South knew winning the Civil War was a very long shot.

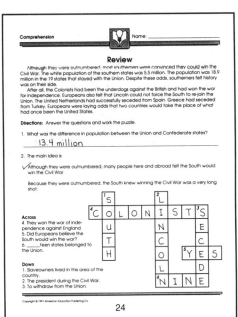

Across
4. They won the war of independence against England. — COLONISTS
5. Did Europeans believe the South would win the war? — YES
6. _____ teen states belonged to the Union. — NINE

Down
1. Slaveowners lived in this area of the country. — SOUTH
2. The president during the Civil War. — LINCOLN
3. To withdraw from the Union. — SECEDE

Fun With Photography

The word photography means "writing with light." "Photo" is from the Greek word *photos* which means light. "Graphy" is from the Greek word *graphic* which means writing. Cameras don't literally write pictures of course. Instead, they imprint an image onto a piece of film.

Even the most sophisticated camera is basically a box with a piece of light sensitive film inside a box. The box has a hole at the opposite end from the film. The light enters the box from the hole—the camera's lens—and shines on the surface of the film to create a picture. The picture that's created on the film is the image the camera's lens is pointed toward.

A **lens** is a circle of glass that is thinner at the edges and thicker in the center. The outer edges of the lens collect the light rays and draw them together at the center of the lens.

The **shutter** helps control the amount of light that enters the lens. Too much light will make the picture too light. Too little light will result in a dark picture. Electronic flash—either built into the camera or attached to the top of it—provides light when needed.

Cameras with automatic electronic flashes will provide the additional light automatically. Electronic flashes—or "flashes" as they are often called—require batteries. If your automatic flash or flash attachment quits working, a dead battery is probably the cause.

Directions: Answer the questions about photography.

1. From what language is the word "photography" derived? **Greek**
2. Where is the camera lens thickest? **In the center**
3. What do the outer edges of the lens do? **They collect light**
4. When is a flash needed? **When not enough light is available**
5. What does the shutter do? **Helps control amount of light**

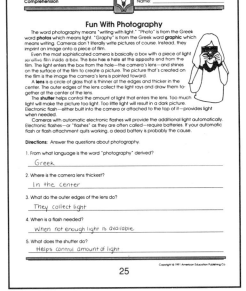

Photography Terms

Like other good professionals, photographers make their craft look easy. Their skill—like that of the graceful ice skater—comes from years of practice. Where skaters develop a sense of balance, photographers develop an "eye" for pictures. They can make important technical decisions about a photograph, or "shooting," a particular scene in the twinkling of an eye.

It's interesting to know some of the technical language that professional photographers use. "Angle of view" refers to the angle from which a photograph is taken. "Depth of field" is the distance between the nearest point and the farthest point in a photo that is in focus.

"Filling the frame" refers to the amount of space the object being photographed takes up in the picture. A close-up picture of a dog, flower or person would fill the frame. A far-away picture would not.

"ASA" refers to the speed of different types of films. "Speed" means the film's sensitivity to light. The letters ASA stand for the American Standards Association. Film manufacturers give their films ratings of 200ASA, 400ASA, etc. to indicate film speed. The higher the number on the film, the higher its sensitivity to light and the faster its speed. The faster the speed, the better it will be at clearly capturing sports images and other action shots.

Directions: Answer the questions about photography terms.

1. Name another term for photographing. **Shooting**
2. This is the distance between the nearest point and the farthest point of a photo that's in focus. **Depth of field**
3. This refers to the speed of different types of film. **ASA rating**
4. A close-up picture of someone's face would
   ☐ provide depth of field ☐ create an ASA ☒ fill the frame
5. To photograph a swimming child, which film speed is better?
   ☐ 200ASA ☒ 400ASA

Photography Puzzler

Directions: Use the facts you have learned about photography to work the puzzle.

Across
2. A film's speed indicates its _____ to light. — SENSITIVITY
5. Good photographers develop an _____ for pictures. — EYE
6. Stands for the American Standards Association. — ASA

Down
1. This is what the Greek word "photos" means. — LIGHT
2. This helps control the amount of light entering the lens. — SHUTTER
3. This term refers to the film's sensitivity to light. — SPEED
4. Would a close-up picture of a cat fill the frame? — YES

Photographing Animals

Animals are a favorite subject of many young photographers. Cats, dogs, hamsters and other pets top the list, followed by zoo animals and the occasional lizard.

Because it's hard to get them to sit still and "perform on command," many professional photographers joke that—given a choice—they will refuse to photograph pets or small children. There are ways around the problem of short attention spans, however.

One way to get an appealing portrait of a cat or dog is to hold a biscuit or other food above the camera. The animal's longing look toward the food will be captured by the camera as a soulful gaze.

Because it's above the camera—out of the camera's range—the treat won't appear in the picture. When you show the picture to your friends afterwards they will be impressed by your pet's loving expression.

If you are using fast film, you can take some good, quick shots of pets by simply snapping a picture right after calling their names. You'll get a different expression from your pet using this technique. Depending on your pet's disposition, the picture will capture an inquisitive expression or possibly a look of annoyance—especially if you've awakened Rover from a nap!

To photograph zoo animals, put the camera as close to the animal's cage as possible so you can shoot between the bars or wire mesh. Wild animals don't respond the same way as pets—after all, they don't "know you"—so you will have to be more patient to capture a good shot. If it's legal to feed the animals, you can get their attention by having a friend toss them treats as you concentrate on shooting some good pictures.

Directions: Answer the questions about photographing animals.

1. Why do some professionals dislike photographing animals? **Because of animals short attention spans**
2. What speed film should you use to photograph quick-moving pets? **Fast film**
3. To capture a pet's loving expression, hold this out of camera range. **Treat**
4. For a good picture of zoo animals
   ☒ get close to the cage ☐ stand back from the cage
5. To get a zoo animal's attention, who should toss them treats?
   ☐ the photographer ☒ a friend ☐ a zoo keeper

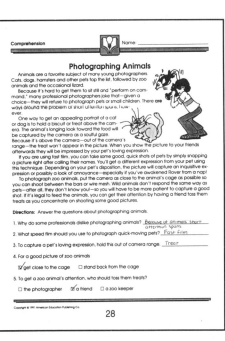

Generalization

A generalization is a statement of principle that applies in many different situations.

Directions: Read each passage and circle the valid generalization.

1. Most people can quickly be taught to use a simple camera. However, it takes time, talent and a good eye to learn to take professional quality photographs. Patience is another quality that good photographers must possess. Those who photograph nature often will wait hours to get just the right light or shadow in their pictures.

   a. There's no one who can't learn to use a camera.
   b. Any patient person can become a good photographer.
   c. (Good photographers have a good eye for pictures.)

2. Photographers such as Diane Arbus, who photograph strange or odd people, also must wait for just the right picture. Many "people photographers" stake out a busy city sidewalk and study the faces of crowds. Then they must leap up quickly and ask to take a picture—or sneakily take one without being observed. Either way, it's not an easy task!

   a. Staking out a busy city sidewalk is a boring task.
   b. ("People photographers" must be patient people and good observers.)
   c. Sneak photography is not a nice thing to do to strangers.

3. Whether the subject is nature or humans, many photographers insist that dawn is the best time to take pictures. The light is clear at this early hour, and mist may still be in the air. The mist gives these early morning photos a haunting, "other world" quality that is very appealing.

   a. (Morning mist gives an unusual quality to most outdoor photographs.)
   b. Photographers all agree that dawn is the best time to take pictures.
   c. Misty light is always important in taking all pictures.

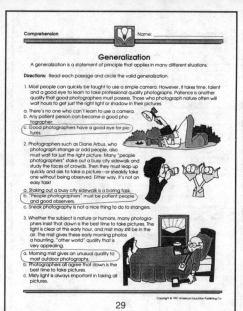

Generalization

Directions: Read each passage and circle the valid generalization.

1. Professional photographers know it's important to keep their cameras clean and in good working order. Amateur photographers should make sure theirs are, too. However, to take good care of your camera, you must first understand the equipment. Camera shop owners say at least half the "defective" cameras people bring in simply need to have the battery changed!

   a. Cameras are delicate and require constant care so they will work properly.
   b. (Many problems amateurs have are caused by lack of familiarity with their equipment.)
   c. Amateur photographers don't know how their cameras work.

2. Once a year, some people take their cameras to a shop to be cleaned. Most never have them cleaned at all! Those who know how can clean their cameras themselves. To avoid scratching the lens, they should use the special cloths and tissues professionals rely on. Amateurs are warned never to unloosen screws, bolts or nuts inside the camera.

   a. (The majority of amateur photographers never bother to have their cameras cleaned.)
   b. Cleaning a camera can be tricky and should be left to professionals.
   c. It's hard to find the special cleaning cloths professionals use.

3. Another simple tip from professionals—make sure your camera works **before** you go on vacation. They suggest taking an entire roll of film and having it developed before your trip. That way, if necessary, you'll have time to have the lens cleaned or other repairs made.

   a. (Check out your camera beforehand to make sure it's in good working order before you travel.)
   b. Vacation pictures are often disappointing because the camera needs repairing.
   c. Take at least one roll of film along on every vacation.

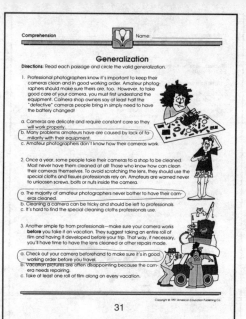

Camera Care

Camera dealers say many amateur photographers should take better care of their cameras. Too often, people carelessly leave expensive cameras laying out where young children or pets can get hold of them. They fail to keep put cameras back into the carrying cases that protect them. They take them to the beach and leave them laying in the sand. Another way people ruin their cameras is by leaving them for days inside a hot car.

Because they must carry so many attachments, professional photographers keep their cameras inside a large, soft shoulder bag. The bag provides extra protection for the camera, which is also protected by its camera case.

Inside the bag are compartments for film, extra lenses and other attachments. Other equipment inside a professional photographer's bag may include the following: lens hood, cable release, filters and holder, cleaning cloth and screw driver. A photographer's bag is filled with all sorts of interesting things!

Flashlights, pens, tape and sometimes a sandwich for lunch may fill out the odd assortment of objects. In addition, many photographers carry a tripod to set the camera on for still pictures. Can you see why photographers usually develop strong arm and shoulder muscles?

Directions: Answer the questions about caring for and storing cameras.

1. Name four ways people abuse their cameras.
   1. Leave them out
   2. don't use case.
   3. leave them out on beach
   4. leave them in hot car

2. What do professional photographers carry their equipment in?
   A large soft shoulder bag

3. Which of the following is **not** in a photographer's bag?
   ☐ lens hood   ☒ tripod   ☐ lens filters

4. Photographers often develop which set of muscles?
   ☐ legs and feet   ☒ arms and shoulders   ☐ head and neck

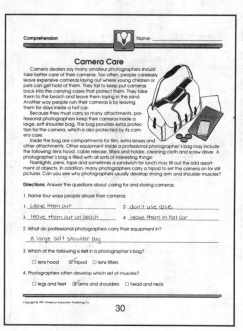

Review

Using A Darkroom

The room where photographs are developed is called a "darkroom." Can you guess why? The room must be completely dark so that light does not get on the film as it is being developed. Because of the darkness and the chemicals used in the developing process, it's important to follow certain darkroom safety procedures.

To avoid shocks while in the darkroom, never touch light switches with wet hands. To avoid touching chemicals, use tongs to transfer prints from one chemical solution to another. When finished with the chemicals, put them back in their bottles. Never leave chemicals out in trays once the developing process is completed.

To avoid skin irritation from chemicals, wipe down all counter tops and surfaces when finished. Another sensible precaution—make sure you have everything you need **before** exposing the film to begin the developing process. Any light that enters the darkroom as you leave to get a forgotten item can ruin the pictures being developed.

Directions: Answer the questions about using a darkroom.

1. Which generalization is correct?
   a. Developing pictures is a time-consuming and difficult process.
   b. It's dangerous to develop pictures in a darkroom.
   c. (Sensible safety procedures are important for darkroom work.)

2. Give directions for working with photography chemicals.
   Use tongs, put them back when done, wipe counters

3. Give the most important detail on how to make sure pictures aren't ruined in the darkroom.
   Don't open the door!

Spelling and Writing Name: _____

Review

Directions: Follow the instructions to see how much you remember from the previous lessons. Can you finish this page correctly without looking back at the other lessons?

1. Write three words that have the /ûr/ sound.

   _____

2. Now write three words that have the /ôr/ sound.

   _____

3. Finish this sentence with a simile:

   My bedroom is as neat as _____

4. Finish this sentence with a metaphor:

   My first day at school this year was _____

5. Use a synonym for crisis in a sentence.

   _____

6. Create a "word picture" based on this sentence:

   The little boy washed his hands.

   _____

   _____

7. Write two or three sentences describing what a person who is worried about taking a test might look like and do. Show how the person feels without using the word "worried."

   _____

   _____

   _____

8. Rewrite this sentence, using an **-ing** form for the verb and the plural form of tornado:

   The winds from the tornado destroyed the trailer park.

   _____

Spelling Words With /kw/, /ks/, And /gz/

The consonant **q** is always followed by **u** in words and pronounced /**kw**/. The letter **x** can be pronounced /**ks**/ as in mi**x**, but when **x** is followed by a vowel, it is usually pronounced /**gz**/ as in e**x**ample.

Directions: Use words from the word box in these exercises.

expense	exist	aquarium	acquire	request
exact	expand	exit	quality	excellent
quiz	quantity	exhibit	expression	squirm

1. Write each word in the row that names one of its sounds. (Hint: the **h** in exhibit is silent.)

/kw/ _____

_____

/ks/ _____

/gz/ _____

2. Finish each sentence with a word that has the sound given. Use each word from the word box only once.

We went to the zoo to see the fish /gz/ _____ .

I didn't know its /gz/_____ location, so we followed the map.

The zoo plans to /kw/_____ some sharks for

its /kw/_____ .

Taking care of sharks is a big /ks/_____ , but a number of people

have asked the zoo to /ks/_____ its display of fish.

These people want a better /kw/_____ of fish,

not a bigger /kw/_____ of them.

I think the zoo already has an /ks/_____ display.

Some of its rare fish no longer /gz/_____ in the ocean.

Spelling and Writing Name: _____

Writing Free Verse

Poems that don't rhyme and don't have a regular rhythm are called "free verse." They often use adjectives, adverbs, similes, and metaphors to create word pictures like this one:

My Old Cat

Curled on my bed at night,
Quietly happy to see me,
Soft, sleepy, relaxed,
A calm island in my life.

Directions: Write your own free verse poems on the topics given.

1. Write a two-line free verse poem about a feeling. Compare it to some kind of food. For example, anger could be a tangle of spaghetti. Give your poem a title.

_____
_____

2. Think of how someone you know is like a color, sunny like yellow, for example. Write a two-line free verse poem on this topic without naming the person. Don't forget a title.

_____
_____

3. Write a four-line free verse poem, like "My Old Cat" above, that creates a word picture of a day at school.

_____
_____
_____
_____

4. Now write a four-line free verse poem about dreaming at night.

_____
_____
_____
_____

5. Write one more four-line free verse poem, this time about your family.

_____
_____
_____
_____

Spelling and Writing  Name: _____

Analyzing Words And Their Parts

Remember that a syllable is a word or part of a word with only one vowel sound.

Directions: Use the words from the word box in these exercises.

expense	exist	aquarium	acquire	request
exact	expand	exit	quality	excellent
quiz	quantity	exhibit	expression	squirm

1. Fill in any missing syllables in these words. Then write the number of syllables in each word.

ex_____lent ( )   ac_____( )   _____quest ( )   _____squirm ( )

quali_____( )   ex_____it ( )   _____act ( )   _____ it ( )

_____pense ( )   _____quiz ( )   ex_____sion ( )   _____ pand ( )

_____quar_____um ( )   _____ist ( )   quan_____ty ( )

2. Write the word that rhymes with each of these words and phrases.

fizz _____   worm _____   the sand _____

resist _____   my best _____   the fence _____

in fact _____   good fit _____   on fire _____

made for me _____   reflection _____

it's been sent _____   this is it _____

3. Write in the word that belongs to the same word family as the one underlined.

I know <u>exactly</u> what I want; I want those ____ shoes.   _____

Those shoes look <u>expensive</u>. Can we afford that ____ ?   _____

She wanted us to <u>express</u> ourselves, but she still didn't like my ____ . _____

When we went to the <u>exhibition</u>, I liked the train ____ best.   _____

The museum has a new <u>acquisition</u>. I wonder what they ____ .   _____

Spelling and Writing

Name: _____

Writing Limericks

Limericks are five-line poems that tend to be silly. Certain lines rhyme, and each line usually has either five or eight syllables, like this:

There once was a young man named Fred	(8 syllables)
Whose big muscles went to his head.	(8 syllables)
"I'll make the girls sigh	(5 syllables)
'Cause I'm quite a guy!"	(5 syllables)
But instead the girls all liked Ted!	(8 syllables)

As you can see, all three 8-syllable lines rhyme, and the two 5-syllable lines rhyme.

Directions: Complete the limericks below.

1. There was a young lady from Kent
   Whose drawings were just excellent.
   _____
   _____
   And to the big city she went.

2. I have a pet squirrel named Squirm
   _____
   He ran up a tree
   As far as could be
   _____

3. There once was a boy who yelled, "Fire!"
   _____
   He just did not see
   _____
   _____

4. One day, I saw my reflection
   _____
   _____
   _____
   _____

Spelling and Writing Name: _____

Figuring Out A Crossword Puzzle

Directions: Read each definition and write the word that is defined in the spaces that start with the same number. If you need help with spelling, look in the word box on page 18.

Across
2. To show
5. A test
6. A cost
10. To obtain
11. To go out
13. To ask
15. To live

Down
1. To get bigger
3. A home for fish
4. Just right
7. Really good
8. How good something is
9. On your face
12. An amount
14. To wiggle around

Spelling and Writing Name: _____

Writing Acrostics

An acrostic is a poem written so the first letter of each line spells a word. The poem tells something about the word that is spelled out.

Here's an example:

I n the grass or underground,
N ow and then they fly around.
S lugs and worms and butterflies,
E ach has its own shape and size.
C aterpillars, gnats, a bee,
T ake them all away from me!

Directions: Write your own acrostic poems for the two words below. Then write a third acrostic poem for a word you select. You can make your poems rhyme or not rhyme, like free verse.

S _____
H _____
O _____
E _____
S _____

P _____
H _____
O _____
N _____
E _____

Write an acrostic poem here for the word you selected:

_____
_____
_____
_____
_____

Spelling and Writing Name: _____

Finding The Spelling Mistakes

Directions: Find the spelling mistakes in each paragraph and write the words correctly on the lines. If you need help, look in the word boxes on pages 3, 10, and 18.

Sabrina wanted to aquire a saltwater acquarium. She was worried about the expence, though, so first she did some reseach. She wanted to learn the exxact care saltwater fish need, not just to exsist, but to florish. One sorce said she needed to put water in the aquarium and wait six weeks before she added the fish. "Good greif!" Sabrina thought. She got a kitten from her nieghbor instead.

_____ _____ _____ _____

_____ _____ _____ _____

One stormy day, Mark was babysitting his neice. He happened to obsurve that the sky looked darker than norml. At first he ignorred it, but then he noticed a black cloud exxpand and grow in hieght. Then a tail dropped down from the twisting cloud and siezed a tree! "It's a toranado!" Mark shouted. "Maybe two toranados! This is an emergensy!" For a breef moment Mark wished he hadn't shouted because his niece looked at him with a very frightened expresion. Just then the cieling began to sag as if it had a heavy wieght on it. "This is an excelent time to visit the basement," he told the little girl as calmly as possible.

_____ _____ _____ _____

_____ _____ _____ _____

_____ _____ _____ _____

Just before Mother's Day, Bethany went to a flourist shop to buy some flowers for her mother. "Well, what is your reqest?" the clerk asked. "I don't have much money," Bethany told him. "So make up your mind," he said impatiently. "Do you want quality or quanity?" Bethany wondered if he was giving her a quizz. She tried not to sqwirm as he stared down at her. Finally she said, "I want cortesy," and she headed for the exxit. The next time, she thought, I won't be decieved by a pretty exibit in the store window.

_____ _____ _____ _____

_____ _____ _____ _____

Spelling and Writing Name: _____

Review

Directions: Can you finish this page without looking back at the previous lessons?

1. Write three words that have the /kw/ sound.
_____   _____   _____

2. Write two words that have the /ks/ sound.
_____   _____

3. Write two words that have the /gz/ sound.
_____   _____

4. Write a limerick poem about yourself and your town.
   It might begin like this: "There was a boy from Columbus...." or
   "There once was a girl from Belair...."

_____
_____
_____
_____
_____

5. Write an acrostic poem using the name of someone in your family and telling what you like about this person. Your poem can rhyme, but it doesn't have to. (Be sure to show it to that person.)

_____
_____
_____
_____
_____
_____
_____
_____
_____

Spelling and Writing

Name: _____

Spelling Words With Silent Letters

Some letters in words are not pronounced. The ones you'll practice in this lesson include the **b** as in crum**b**, **l** as in ca**l**m, **n** as in autum**n**, **g** as in desi**g**n, and **h** as in **h**our.

Directions: Use the words from the word box in these exercises.

condemn	yolk	campaign	assign	salmon
hymn	limb	chalk	tomb	foreign
resign	column	spaghetti	rhythm	solemn

1. Write each word in the row with its silent letter.

/n/ _____

/l/ _____

/g/ _____

/b/ _____

/h/ _____

2. Finish these sentences with a word containing the silent letter given. Use each word from the word box only once.

What did the teacher /g/ _____ for homework?

She put words in a /n/ _____ on the board.

When she finished writing, her hands were white with /l/ _____ .

The church choir clapped in /h/ _____ with

the /n/ _____ .

While I was cracking an egg, the /l/ _____ slipped on the floor.

Did the explorers find anything in the ancient /b/ _____ ?

My favorite dinner of all is /h/ _____ .

Don't /n/ _____ me for making one little mistake.

Spelling and Writing Name: _____

Organizing Paragraphs

A topic sentence tells the main idea of a paragraph and is usually the first sentence. Support sentences follow it, providing details about the topic.

Directions: Arrange each group of sentences below into a paragraph that makes sense. Write the topic sentence first and underline it. One sentence in each group should not be included in the paragraph, so cross it out.

Now chalk drawings are considered art by themselves.
The earliest chalk drawings were on the walls of caves.
Chalk is also used in cement, fertilizer, toothpaste, and makeup.
Chalk once was used just to make quick sketches.
Chalk has been used for drawing for thousands of years.
Then the artist would paint pictures from the sketches.

_____
_____
_____
_____
_____

Dams also keep young salmon from swimming downriver to the ocean.
Most salmon live in the ocean but return to fresh water to lay their eggs and breed.
Dams prevent salmon from swimming upriver to their spawning grounds.
Pacific salmon die after they spawn the first time.
One kind of fish pass is a series of pools of water that lead the salmon over the dams.
Dams are threatening salmon by interfering with their spawning.
To help with this problem, some dams have special "fish passes" to allow salmon to swim over the dam.

_____
_____
_____
_____
_____
_____
_____

Spelling and Writing Name: _____

Building Paragraphs

Directions:
1. Read each group of questions and the topic sentence.
2. On another sheet of paper, write support sentences that answer each question. Use your imagination!
3. Put your support sentences in order.
4. Read the whole paragraph out loud, make any necessary changes so the sentences fit together, and copy your sentences on this page after the topic sentence.

Questions: Why did Jimmy feel sad?
What happened to change how he felt?
How does he feel when he comes to school now?

Jimmy used to look so solemn when he came to school. _____
_____
_____
_____
_____
_____

Questions: Why did Jennifer want to go to another country?
Why couldn't she go?
Does she have any plans to change that?

Jennifer always wanted to visit a foreign country. _____
_____
_____
_____
_____
_____

Questions: What was Paul's "new way"?
Did anyone else like it?
Did Paul like it himself?

Paul thought of a new way to fix spaghetti. _____
_____
_____
_____
_____
_____

Copyright © 1994 American Education Publishing Co.

Spelling and Writing Name: _____

Matching Subjects And Verbs

If the subject of a sentence is singular, the verb must be singular.

If the subject is plural, the verb should be plural.

Like this:
  S   V
The **dog** with floppy ears **is eating**.
  S   V
The **dogs** in the cage **are eating**.

Directions: Write in the singular or plural form of the subject in each sentence so that it matches the verb. If you need help spelling plural forms, look on page 16.

1. The (yolk) _____ in this egg is bright yellow.

2. The (child) _____ are putting numbers in columns.

3. Both (coach) _____ are resigning at the end of the year.

4. Those three (class) _____ were assigned to the gym.

5. The (lunch) _____ for the children are ready.

6. (Spaghetti) _____ with meatballs is delicious.

7. Where are the (box) _____ of chalk?

8. The (man) _____ in the truck were collecting broken tree limbs.

9. The (rhythm) _____ of that music is just right for dancing.

10. Sliced (tomato) _____ on lettuce are good with salmon.

11. The (announcer) _____ on TV was condemning the dictator.

12. Two (woman) _____ are campaigning for mayor of our town.

13. The (group) _____ of travelers was on its way to three foreign countries.

14. The (choir) _____ of thirty children is singing hymns.

15. In spite of the parade, the (hero) _____ were solemn.

Spelling and Writing Name: _____

Explaining With Examples

Some paragraphs describe people, places, or events using adjectives, adverbs, similes, and metaphors, like the paragraphs you wrote on page 15. Other paragraphs explain by naming examples, like this one:

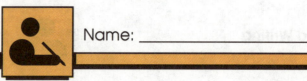

Babysitting is not an easy way to earn money. For example, the little girl you're watching may be extra cranky and cry until her parents come home. Or maybe, the family didn't leave any snacks and you have to starve all night. Even worse, the child could fall and get hurt. Then you have to decide whether you can take care of her yourself or you need to call for help. No, babysitting isn't easy.

Directions: Write the rest of the paragraph for each topic sentence below, using examples to explain what you mean.
1. If the topic sentence gives a choice, select one.
2. Write your examples on another sheet of paper.
3. Read them over and put them in order.
4. When the sentences are the way you want them, copy them below.

Sometimes dreams can be scary.
_____
_____
_____
_____
_____
_____
_____

You can learn a lot by living in a foreign country.
_____
_____
_____
_____
_____
_____
_____

Copyright © 1994 American Education Publishing Co.

Spelling and Writing Name: _____

Making Nouns Possessive

A possessive noun owns something.

To make a singular noun possessive, add an apostrophe and **s**: mayor**'s** campaign.

To make a plural noun possessive when it already ends with **s**, just add an apostrophe: dogs**'** tails.

To make a plural noun possessive when it doesn't end with **s**, add an apostrophe and **s**: men**'s** shirts.

Directions: Write in the correct form of the word given for each sentence in that group. Be careful, though. Sometimes the word will need to be singular, sometimes plural, sometimes singular possessive, and sometimes plural possessive.

Like this: teacher

How many ____teachers____ does your school have?

Where is the ____teacher's____ coat?

All the ____teachers'____ mailboxes are in the school office.

1. **reporter**

   Two _____ were assigned to the story.

   One _____ car broke down on the way to the scene.

   The other _____ was riding in the car, which had to be towed away.

   Both _____ notes ended up missing.

2. **child**

   The _____ are hungry.

   How much spaghetti can one _____ eat?

   Put this much on each _____ plate.

   The _____ spaghetti is ready for them.

3. **mouse**

   Some _____ made a nest under those boards.

   I can see the _____ hole from here.

   A baby _____ has wandered away from the nest.

   The _____ mother is coming to get it.

Spelling and Writing

Name: _____

Review

Directions: See if you can complete these exercises without looking back at the previous lessons.

1. Write two words with a silent **l**.

   _____

2. Write two words with a silent **n**.

   _____

3. Write two words with a silent **g**.

   _____

4. Write a word with a silent **b** and one with a silent **h**.

   _____

5. Write a paragraph that explains why insects can be a nuisance at a picnic. Include several examples of how they can get in the way. First, write your paragraph on another sheet of paper. Then make any needed changes, be sure your topic sentence is first, and copy your paragraph below.

   _____
   _____
   _____
   _____
   _____

6. Finish this analogy, using a word with a silent **l**:

   Fly is to **eagle** as **swim** is to_____.

7. Write a sentence with a plural subject and a plural verb and include the word solemn.

   _____
   _____

8. Write a sentence with a plural possessive noun and include the word foreign.

   _____
   _____

9. Find four misspelled words below and write them correctly.
   The teacher wrote the words for a hym on the board with chak. She assined me to clap the rhythem while the others sang.